# Little Girl, Big Challenge!

For Piper,

"Believe in yourself..."

Phil Boyd

## Written by Phillip Boyd
## Illustrated by Reece Mingard

For little S.B.
A story inspired by your beautiful sister & brother.
We love you forever.
P.B.

Written by Phillip Boyd
Illustrated by Reece Mingard
ISBN: 9798849747491

# Little Girl, Big Challenge!

One bright and very sunny day
little Audrey went to the park
with her daddy.

There were seesaws, swings and slides, however
it was the monkey bars that excited her the most.

But these were no ordinary monkey bars,
these were magical rainbow monkey bars.
And Audrey loved, loved, loved magical rainbows!

Little Audrey looked up at the big, big, big challenge ahead and said,
"I'll swing like a little monkey until I get to the end!"

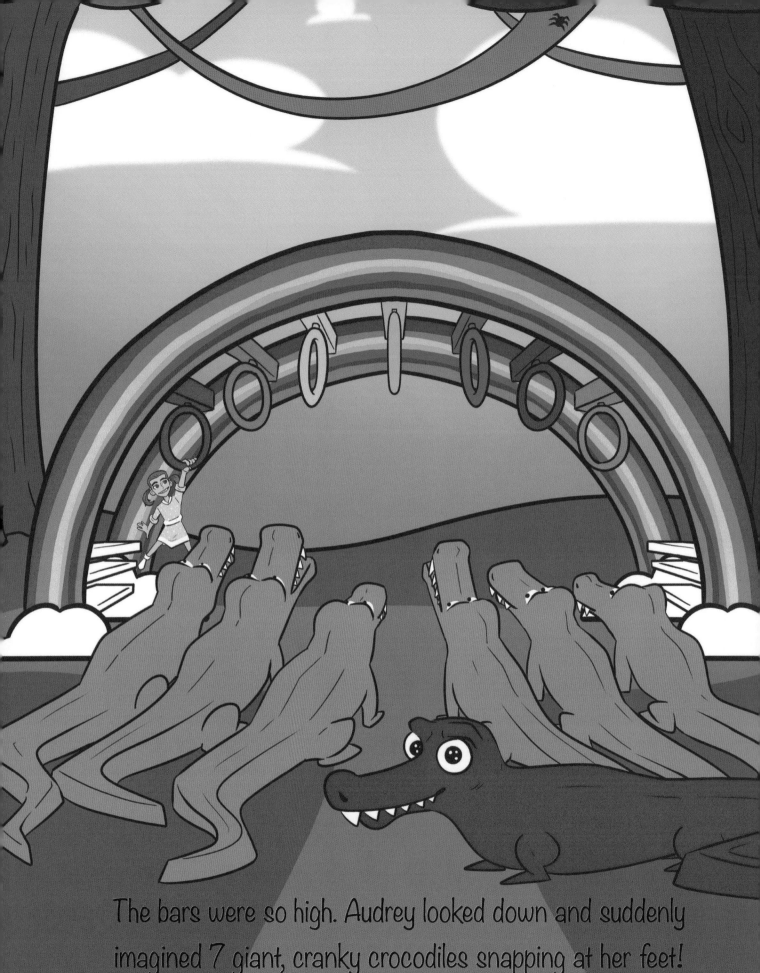

The bars were so high. Audrey looked down and suddenly imagined 7 giant, cranky crocodiles snapping at her feet! (Can you spot the smiling red crocodile on this page?)

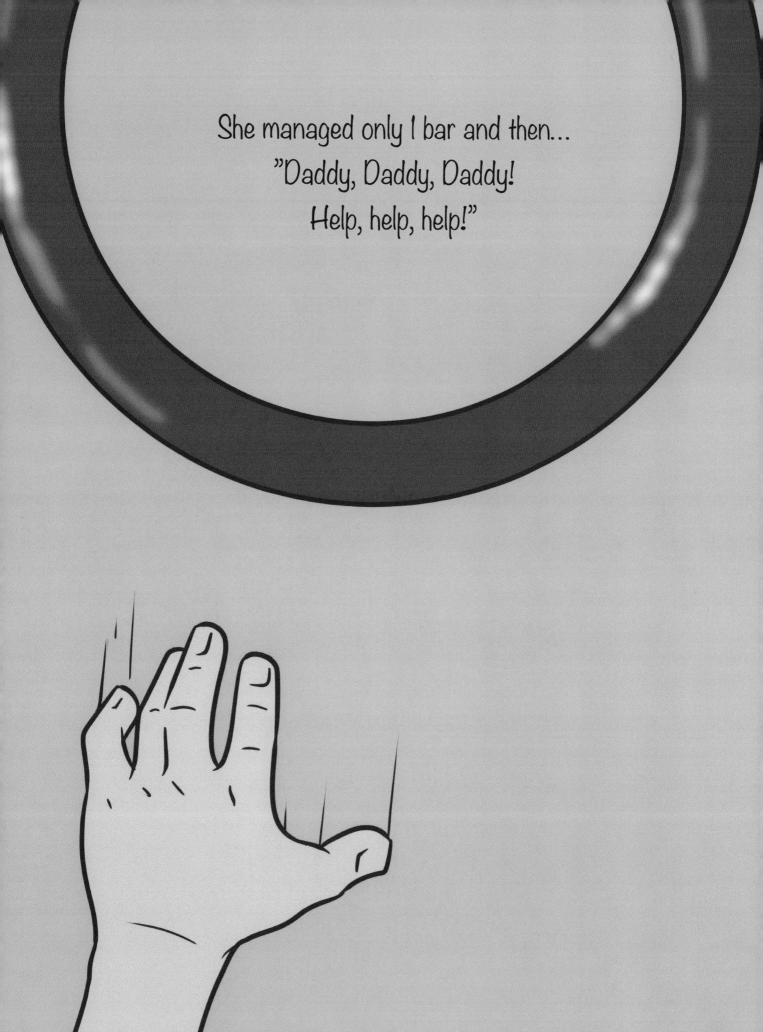

Another week and it was back, back, back to the park.
This time Audrey looked down and imagined
6 slimy, smelly, pumping, trumping toads!
(Can you spot the smiling orange toad on this page?)

Another week and it was back, back, back to the park.
This time Audrey looked down and imagined 5 snotty,
sneezing sharks swimming in a snot filled swamp!
(Can you spot the smiling yellow shark on this page?)

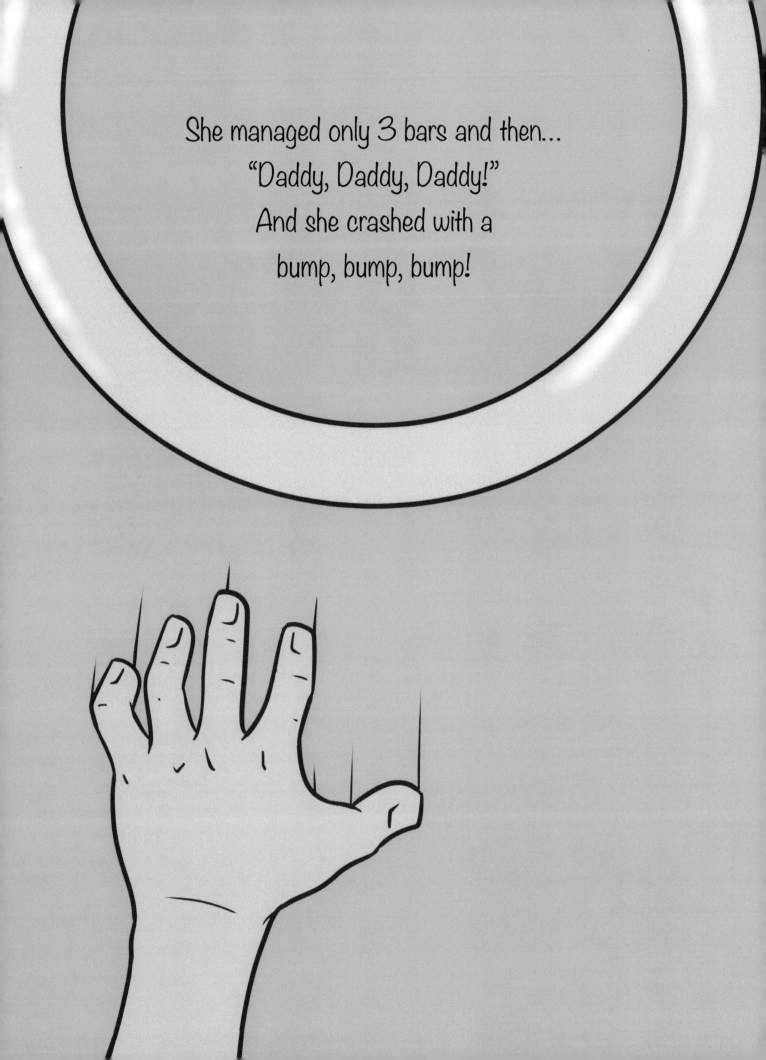

Another week and it was back, back, back to the park.
This time Audrey looked down and imagined 4 big,
snarling, gnarling tigers prowling below her!
(Can you spot the smiling green tiger on this page?)

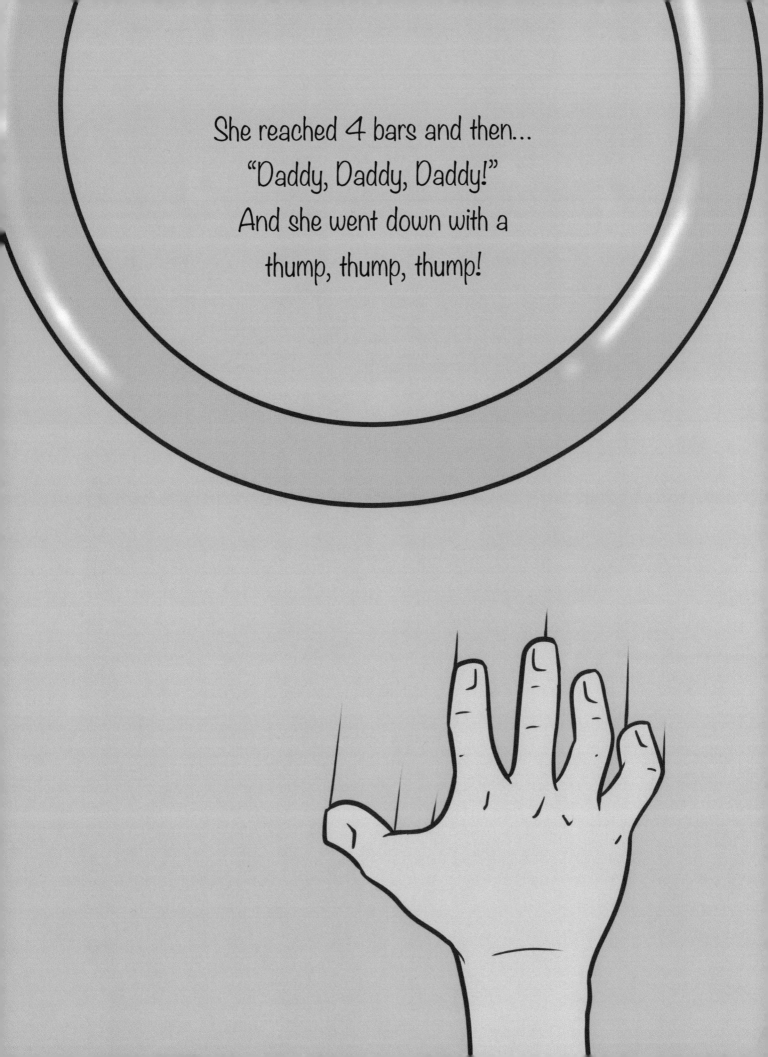

She reached 4 bars and then...
"Daddy, Daddy, Daddy!"
And she went down with a
thump, thump, thump!

Another week and it was back, back, back to the park.
This time Audrey looked down and imagined 3 huge,
hairy spiders spinning spindly, sparkly webs everywhere!
(Can you spot the smiling blue spider on this page?)

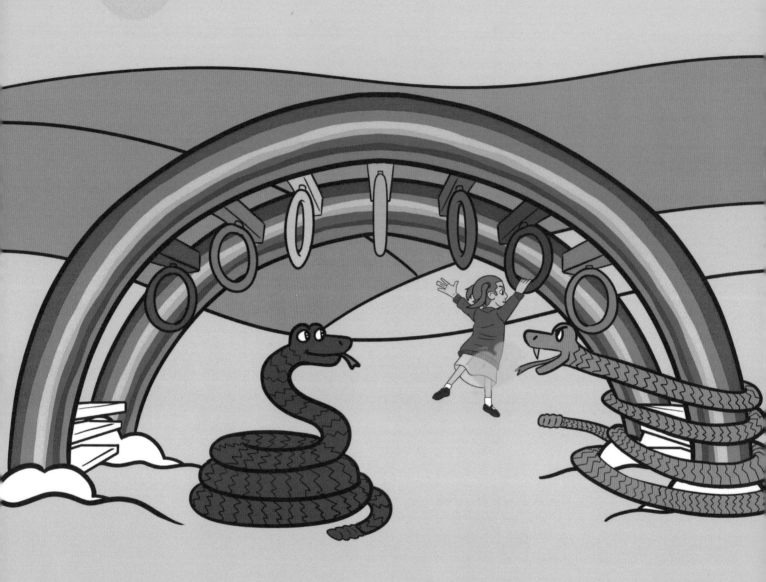

Another week and it was back, back, back to the park.
This time Audrey looked down and imagined 2 slurping,
burping snakes slithering slowly beneath her!
(Can you spot the smiling indigo snake on this page?)

Another week and it was back, back, back to the park.
Audrey looked down and imagined a smiling flamingo with its
beautiful violet wings spread below her feet.
"Believe in yourself," whispered Daddy.

Audrey took a deep, deep, deep breath.
1 bar, then 2, 3 bars, then 4, 5 bars,
then 6, 7 bars and then...
"Daddy, Daddy, Daddy!"
And she finished with a
"Whoop, whoop, whoop!"

Everyone was cheering and everyone was applauding,
including the creatures who had been smiling and supporting!
Audrey's little brothers were there too,
smiling and waving,
completing the crew.

So, after weeks of practise, practise, practise
Audrey was a little girl who had become a little monkey!
A little girl who had faced her fears,
taking on a big, big, big challenge without any tears.

She had dared to believe in herself and was unstoppable,

because if you believe in yourself...

anything is possible.

Printed in Great Britain
by Amazon

20603359R00016